Turtle and Snake and the Christmas Tree

by Kate Spohn

VIKING

To Melanie

VIKING
Published by the Penguin Group
Penguin Putnam Books for Young Readers, 345 Hudson Street,
New York, New York 10014, U.S.A.

Penguin Books Ltd, Registered Offices: Harmondsworth, Middlesex, England

First published by Viking and Puffin books,
divisions of Penguin Putnam Books for Young Readers, 2000

1 3 5 7 9 10 8 6 4 2

LIBRARY OF CONGRESS CATALOGING-IN-PUBLICATION DATA
Spohn, Kate.
Turtle and Snake and the Christmas tree / by Kate Spohn.
p. cm.
"Puffin Books."
Summary: Turtle and Snake are ready to decorate a Christmas tree but
they first need to find the perfect tree.
ISBN 0-670-88867-2 (hardcover) — ISBN 0-14-130968-7 (pbk.)
[1. Christmas trees—Fiction. 2. Christmas—Fiction.
3.Turtles—Fiction. 4. Snakes—Fiction.] I. Title.
PZ7.S7636 Ts 2000   [E]—dc21   00-008186

Printed in Hong Kong
Set in Bookman

Viking® and Easy-to-Read® are registered trademarks of Penguin Putnam Inc.

Reading Level 1.5

Turtle and Snake
and the
Christmas Tree

Look at all the snow!
It's a perfect day to
pick out a Christmas tree.

Let's go, Turtle.
Let's go, Snake.

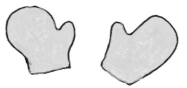

Put on your mittens.

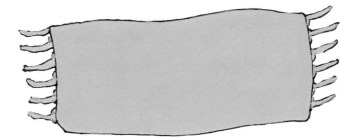

Put on your scarf.

Put on your hat.

All ready!

Where will we find a tree?
At the tree farm!

Down,
down the hill!
Down the hill to the tree farm.

We're ready to pick out a tree.

Snake likes the thin tree.
Too thin!

Turtle likes the wide tree.
Too wide!

18

Snake likes the tall tree.
Too tall!

Turtle likes
the short tree.
Too short!

"Too picky!" says the tree farmer.
No tree!

Turtle and Snake go home.
Up, up the hill.

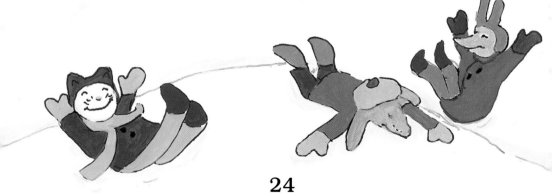

What's that?
Could it be?

Not too thin.

Not too wide.

Not too tall.

Not too short.

It's a perfect Christmas tree!

Let's trim the tree!

Get the candy canes.

Get the balls.

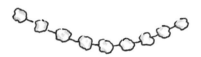

Get the popcorn.

Get the star.

Everybody helps.

Merry Christmas, Turtle!
Merry Christmas, Snake!
Merry Christmas, everybody!